Marie Joussaye

The Songs that Quinte Sang

Marie Joussaye

The Songs that Quinte Sang

ISBN/EAN: 9783744767514

Printed in Europe, USA, Canada, Australia, Japan

Cover: Foto ©Andreas Hilbeck / pixelio.de

More available books at **www.hansebooks.com**

The

Songs

That

Quinte Sang

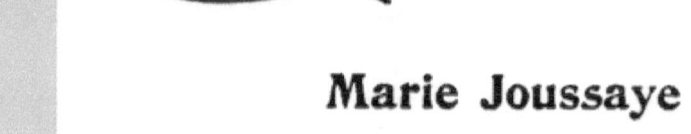

Marie Joussaye

BELLEVILLE, CANADA.
SUN PRINTING AND PUBLISHING COMPANY.
1895.

CONTENTS.

NOTE—The sketch illustrating the lines " Dear hearts, their sleep is calm aud sweet by Quinte's restful side," is from the pen of the late Stewart Hunter, who died a few days after making the sketch.

By Quinte's Side.

DEAR comrades of a vanished past,
　My childhood's playmates, kind and true,
Who dwell on Quinte's sunlit shore,
　I give these songs to you.

Old Quinte sang them in my ears
　Long years ago, when I was young.
I give them back in later years
　The songs that Quinte sung.

How often when a child I strayed
　Dear Quinte's peaceful shores along,
My heart and soul responding to
　The music of her song.

The wild bird oft would hush its song
　Whilst skimming by on outspread wing
And listen while old Quinte taught
　Her poet child to sing.

And this the sum of all she taught,
　As tranquilly she flowed along,
Through all these years I've not forgot,
　"Live, suffer and be strong."

Though but a child I understood,
　Why Quinte sang that song to me,
And my young heart was hushed and soothed
　By her sweet minstrelsy.

And some have chided me, because
  The songs I love to write are sad,
They bid me sing in blither strains
  And make the world more glad.

I heed them not, the harp responds
  Unto my touch with plaintive ring
And, like the birds, I sing the songs
  That God hath bid me sing.

If every bird sang as the lark
  Their blithesome notes would mock the ear,
The thrush's song is not less sweet,
  Although we weep to hear.

And though we love the sunshine well
  We would not have it always day,
Man soon would weary were his life
  One ceaseless roundelay.

You will not chide my mournful songs
  O kindly friends of bygone years!
Because you know my early days
  Knew less of smiles than tears.

And whether critics praise or blame
  I know that loving eyes will note
And kindly voices praise the songs
  For love of her who wrote.

Let greater poets strive for bays,
  My heart would throb with truer pride
At one kind word of honest praise
  From friends by Quinte's side.

O, friends and playmates of the past,
  Who dwell on Quinte's sunlit shore,
Across the gulf that time has wrought
  I greet you all once more!

Though new-found friends have smiled on me
  My heart has never swerved from you
The old-time friends must ever be
  Far dearer than the new.

The joys that made your kind hearts glad
  Have waked an answering chord in mine
And ye have wept when I was sad
  My friends of " Auld Lang Syne."

Through all these weary, waiting years
  For your dear faces I have yearned
And oft through mists of blinding tears
  My longing eyes have turned

Back to the well-loved childhood's haunts,
  Where dear old Quinte, calm and mild,
With sunny smiles of welcome waits
  To greet her absent child.

I miss some faces that I loved
  Their feet have sought a foreign shore.
May Heaven turn their wandering steps
  To Quinte's side once more.

And some, grown weary of this life,
  Have folded their pale hands and died.
Dear hearts, their sleep is calm and sweet
  By Quinte's restful side.

And ye who stood above their graves,
  Your saddened hearts with anguish torn,
And deemed the burden Heaven sent,
  Too heavy to be borne

Have learned at last, as I once learned,
  The burden of old Quinte's song
That life's great lesson is " to live,
  To suffer, and be strong."

O, friends of vanished childhood's days
  Who dwell on Quinte's sunlit shore,
Across the intervening years
  I greet you all once more

Whilst all my heart goes out in prayer,
  May peace and joy with you abide
And God be with the friends who dwell
  By pleasant Quinte's side.

" Dear hearts, their sleep is calm and sweet
  By Quinte's restful side."

Rest After Pain.

The patient, suffering heart is hushed and still
   And he has gained eternal rest at last,
All care is over now, all weariness,
          All pain is past.

Not as a foe, but as a friend Death came,
   Bearing the gift of peace in his pale hand ;
He touched the tortured heart and anguish fled
          At his command.

Rest, weary one, and be thou not afraid,
   Death guards thee well, no agonizing dart
Can pierce the icy shield his hand has laid
          Above thy heart.

Sleep, well-beloved, no harm can come to thee,
   For all is peace within that " low green tent,"
Sleep, and enjoy the long desired rest
          That Heaven sent.

If I Had Known.

If I had known how steep the path of **Fame,**
   How long the weary years of toil and care,
How sharp **the** sting of poverty, the shame
   Of **baffled hopes,** the bitter, wild dispair
Of prayers unanswered, **ever backward** thrust
   Upon my heart like ashes, dust on dust,
I never would have **ventured all alone**
   To tread the rugged path, **if I had known.**

If I had known **how soon** love's roses **fade,**
   How **soon their bloom and** beauty know **eclipse,**
A cluster o'er my heart I had not laid,
   Nor **touched** the fragrant blossoms with **my lips,**
And my poor heart and lips had **not been torn**
   If I had **known** love's rose concealed a thorn,
Which rankled sore long after **Love** had flown,
   I had not suffered so, **if I had known.**

If I had **known** that friendship had a sting,
   That **smiling** lips and eyes could hide deceit,
I had not **crowned or** worshiped **as** a king
   This poor clay idol, shattered at my **feet,**
Nor given all my loyal trust to learn
   The friend I loved but mocked me in return.
Over its broken hopes my heart makes **moan,**
   I had not **trusted** so, if I had known.

If I had known, nay heart, why should I mourn ?
  Better by far I did not know the pain
Fate had allotted me e'er I was born.
  And who shall say my life has been in vain?
Life is made up of equal joy and care,
  The joy I missed hath been another's share
And every burden added to my load
  Hath eased some other comrade on the road;
And God knew best, before the griefs now flown
  My courage would have failed if I had known.

Some Day.

Some day when I have conned the page of pain
So closely that no lesson will remain
For me to learn, and when my lips have quaffed
Unto the dregs, pale sorrow's bitter druaght,
Then will this troubled heart, so sorely tried,
From earthly eare and tormoil find release
And death will grant me all that life denied,
Rest and oblivion and unbroken peace.

Oh ! longed-for hour, when I shall calmly rest
With idle hands crossed over pulseless breast
All peacefully within my narrow bed,
Unheeding those who weep above my head,
But, Ah ! They would not weep if they could know
How gladly I shall welcome death, and so
Whene'er my sobbing heart makes moan, I say
Hush, hush my heart, the time will come some day.

Waiting.

All day long I walk the shore
  Gazing out across the sea
Where the merry white-capped waves
  Chase each other in their glee.

And I watch with eager eyes,
  Pacing slowly to and fro,
For the ships I sent to sea
    Many weary years ago.

Other ships come sailing in
  From countries strange far away
And with canvas closely furled
  Lie at anchor in the bay.

And the sailors as they pass
  Answer me right cheerily
When I ask them of my ships
  That are still far out at sea.

Oh! I know they pity me,
  Keeping vigil on the strand,
And with words of kindly cheer
  Come and take me by the hand.

And they bid me cease to weep,
  " Weep no more, dear heart," they say,
" Soon you'll see your bonnie ships
  Anchored safely in the bay."

So I dry my tears and stand
Gazing out across the main,
And with patience wait the hour
When my ships will come again.

Some day I shall see them all
Anchored safely off the shore,
Then my heart will cease to mourn,
And my vigils will be o'er.

Just so sure as smile the stars
In the mirror of the sea,
Just so sure my bonnie ships
Will return, some day, to me.

My Ships That Went to Sea.

From the haven of the sheltered bay
My ships sailed out in proud array :
'Twas the morn of a golden summer day
      And the wind blew fair and free.
The air was clear, and the sky was bright,
And the blue waves laughed in the glad sunlight
And, Oh ! But it was a goodly sight
      As my ships sailed out to sea.

I was proud of my ships, a gallant fleet,
With their graceful hulls, so trim and neat,
Sturdy and staunch and all complete
      From their spars to the smallest rope.
One was a ship of stately mien
Whose white sails shone with a silver sheen,
A goodlier ship was never seen,
      And I called her " The Golden Hope."

And laden was she with a cargo rare,
With beautiful dreams and fancies fair,
A poet's song and a true heart's prayer,
      And many a smile and tear.
Dreams of wealth, and dreams of fame,
Hopes of winning an honored name
And all the pride of a lofty aim,
      And many a hope and fear.

And I watched them as they sailed afar
'Till I saw the top of each slender spar
Fade beyond the horizon's bar,
　　　　But my heart was light and gay.
For why should I feel a throb of fear
When the wind blew fair and the sky was clear
So my heart was light with hope and cheer　.
　　　　As I watched them sail away,

But often my heart grew sick with fear
For my ships were gone for many a year
And O, but the nights were long and drear
　　　　And the days dragged wearily,
And often when others were fast asleep
And the angry storm king rode the deep,
The whole night long I would watch and weep
　　　　For my bonnie ships at sea.

But they bring me glad, good news to-day,
" Oh ! Your ships are coming in," they say,
" You can see them gliding up the bay
　　　　In the glow of the morning sun."
Oh ! My ships are in with their cargoes rare
And their colors streaming in the air
My bonnie ships, so brave and fair,
　　　　They are all in—save one.

The Golden Hope with topmasts tall
Rides like a queen among them all,
But a fairy shallop, frail and small,
　　　　The dearest of all to me,
One night when the winds and waves were high
Went down to her doom 'neath a pitiless sky,
And never a thought for the rest have I
　　　　Since Love went down at sea.

Two Roses.

High on a lofty mountain
　One blossomed in beauty **rare,**
The other bloomed in a valley,
　And both **were sweet** and fair.

Bnt **the** longing eyes of the maiden
　Were fixed on the heights above,
" I will gather Fame's fairest roses,
　There is time enough **for Love.**"

And she climbed the rugged mountain
　Though the task was hard and **long,**
Though the path proved steep and weary,
　For her heart was brave and strong.

But the sharp thorns wounded sorely
　As she grasped the longed-for prize,
And she could not see its beauty
　For the tears that dimmed her eyes.

But her heart grew soft and tender
　Amid all her pain **and** woe,
As she thought of the fair, sweet flower
　In the pleasant vale below.

But, alas, even while she tarried
　Far up on the mountain side,
The beautiful rose in the valley
　Had faded away and died.

The Recompense.

The King once sent His messenger to me
  Charged with a message from the court above.
"Ask what thou wilt and it shall granted be."
  And my first prayer was, "Angel! Give me love."

The angel smiled on me, then gently sighed,
  "My child! To such as thee, Love bringeth woe."
But still I prayed and would not be denied,
  Until at last he murmured, "Be it so,"

And held Love's chalice to my eager lips,
  But scarcely had I touched it's golden rim
When all life's brightness suffered swift eclipse
  And sun and stars unto my eyes grew dim.

And on my lips Love's sweetness turned to rue.
  "Oh, Angel!" then I cried, with sobbing breath,
"I asked for Love, Life's sweetest gift, and you
  Have mocked me with the bitterness of Death."

The angel smiled once more, then said, "Not so,
  The sweetness of Love's wine is not for all.
To some it bringeth bliss, to others woe ;
  Upon some lips its honey turns to gall.

But fullest recompense awaits above,
  So be thou comforted, my child, and know
That God reserves His richest meed of Love
  For those who miss its sweetness here below."

Life and Death.

On a bed of pain the sick girl lay
  With closed, white-lidded eyes,
As the sunset gilded the azure bay
  And crimsoned the western skies,
Whilst over her head in bitter strife
Strove the Angel of Death and the Angel of Life.

In and out of the chamber crept
  The watchers, with noiseless tread,
They feared to disturb the one who slept,
  For they knew how frail the thread
That held her light and wavering breath
And balanced her soul between life and death.

Then a gentle voice the silence broke,
  And they gathered around the bed;
In low, sweet accents the sick girl spoke.
  Strange were the words she said :
" Hearken to me and cease the strife,
O Angel of Death and Angel of Life.

" I am weary listening to the strife
  And to end it I am fain,
So cease to struggle, O Death and Life
  And I'll choose between ye twain."
Then turning to Life she wearily sighed,
" Tell me, what gifts can'st thou give thy bride ? "

And swift from his lips the answer came:
　"O maiden! I'll give thee health
And youth and hope and deathless fame,
　And treasures of golden wealth."
Then his voice grew soft as the note of a dove,
"But best of all, I will give thee love."

But she wearily turned her head aside
　As he spake Love's fatal name.
"Thou dost mock my sorrow, O Life!" she cried,
　"For what to me is fame?
And health and wealth prove worthless too,
Since hope is dead and my love untrue.

"O Angel! I spurn thy gifts and thee."
　And she turned to his rival, Death,
"And thou! what hast thou in store for me?"
　She whispered with fleeting breath,
A cool, soft kiss on her brow he pressed,
And murmured, "Oblivion, peace and rest."

And the maiden's face grew strangely calm
　At the sound of the angel's voice,
And she laid her hand in his pale, cold palm.
　Oh! wise was the maiden's choice.
And the watchers in silence held their breath
As her soul went out to the arms of Death.

Messengers to the Dead.

Friends who even now are weeping
  'Round the one you love so well,
Know that sound of human sorrow
  Cannot break Death's mighty spell.
Cease to weep, thy bitter wailing
  Falls upon a deafened ear,
Tears and sobs are unavailing,
  He is dead, he cannot hear.

From a friend who knew and loved him
  Since his earliest childhood's hour,
And who shares your bitter heart ache
  Comes this offering of flowers.
Let their beauty light the shadows
  Death has brought around his bed,
Breathing forth their subtle incense,
  Messengers unto the dead.

Lay them on his pulseless bosom,
  Clasp them in his pale, cold hand,
As they breathe their silent message
  He will know and understand
For their breath is far more subtle
  Than the power of human speech,
And can penetrate his senses
  Where our voices cannot reach.

Tell him, white and fragrant Roses,
 Of our friendship, strong and true ;
Of our deep and heartfelt sorrow,
 Whisper thou, O mournful Rue !
But we leave the tenderest message
 Unto thee, Forget-me-not,
Tell him that through all life's changes
 He will never be forgot.

A. G. C.

Dear child, 'twas vain for me to pray
 That storms might never cloud thy skies,
Or that the tears of anguish may
 Ne'er dim thy bonnie eyes.

For never mortal yet but knew
 The weight of sorrow's crushing thrall,
Joy cometh to a chosen few,
 But sorrow comes to all.

Yet from my heart this prayer goes up,
 When Sorrow's draught your lips must meet,
May Love and Friendship kiss the cup
 And make the bitter sweet.

At the River.

I am standing alone by a mystic tide,
  And the dark swift waters flow past my feet,
While'st floating across from the other side
  Come strains of music, heavenly sweet,
And I see the beautiful white-robed throng
  Beckoning to me across the wave,
And I long to join in the rapturous song,
  But the cold, dark waters I dare not brave.

I press my feet to the River of Death,
  But backward shrink with quivering start
For the icy waters have stopped my breath
  And frozen the blood in my frightened heart,
Then softly and sweetly the angel song
  Comes floating across to my listening ear :
"Though the river is dark and swift and strong,
  There is one who will help you, so be of good cheer."

And then in the midst of the beautiful throng
  A wondrous vision bursts on my sight :
I seem to see on that shining strand
  A form of celestial glory and light,
And softly there steals to my troubled soul
  Those loving words that calm all fear:
"Fear not, my child, though the river be cold
  I will bear thee up, so be of good cheer."

With a world of love in his patient eyes
  He stretches the wounded hands to aid,
And once more speaks in such sad surprise :
  "Oh doubting one, art thou still afraid?
My feet once pressed the cold dark wave,
  Unaided I stepped o'er the river's brink,
And wil't thou not trust me. its dangers brave?
  I will bear thee up and thou can'st not sink."

Then all fear goes out from my doubting soul
  And a wondrous peace steals in instead,
As once more I press to the river cold
  And the icy waters no longer dread,
And as boldly I plunge in the chilling tide
  The song of the Angels rings sweet and clear—
"Though the river is dark and cold and wide
  Thy Saviour is with thee, so be of good cheer."

The Sailor's Grave.

A stately ship sails out to sea,
And her sailors sing right merrily
As they cheerily hoist the snowy sail
Which bends before the freshning gale.

But there is one who stands apart,
For song and jest he has no heart,
And his eyes are dim with unshed tears
As the fading shore slow disappears.

Now 'tis lost to sight, he breathes a sigh,
" My own, dear native land, good bye,
Farewell, loved ones on yonder shore
We part to meet, perchance no more."

*   *   *   *   *   *   *   *   *   *

The ocean rests in slumber grand,
And the ship is far out from the land ;
All gilded in the radiant beams
Of the golden sun, her white sail gleams.

On the good ship's deck the sailors pace,
A solemn fear on every face.
A stranger grim with chilling breath
Has come on board, his name is Death.

O brave young heart ! that undismayed
Shrank not when death's chill hand was laid
Upon thy lips, stilling their breath
Sealing them with the seal of death.

With canvas coarse for winding sheet
They shrouded him from head to feet,
Brushed from his brow the curls of gold,
And crossed his hands on his bosom cold.

Then a prayer was murmured low and soft,
While the rising winds in the shrouds aloft
Sang a mournful requiem, slow and sad—
A funeral dirge for the sailor lad.

Then a sob broke forth from each manly breast
As he slowly sank 'neath the blue wave's crest ;
O noble heart ! so true and brave,
Sleep on in rest in your sailor's grave.

Sleep on and fear no earthly harm,
Sleep ! till the judgment's dread alarm
Shall wake thee from thy dreamless sleep
And call thee from the silent deep.

*　　*　　*　　*　　*　　*　　*　　*　　*　　*　　*

And the years roll on in grief and joy,
And a mother weeps for her fair-haired boy,
And a sister prays with a sob and tear
For the safe return of her brother dear.

And a maiden stands in a cottage door
Listening for a step that will come no more,
And she prays as she looks across the sea,
" God speed my darling back to me."

And when at eve in the glowing west
The golden sun sinks down to rest
They often watch the fading light
And say, " Perhaps he will come to-night."

Ah ! faithful hearts ! 'tis all in vain,
Your loved one will not come again.
Far, far away 'neath the rolling wave
He sleeps alone in a sailor's grave.

By the Sea.

On the cold, gray shore I walk alone
  Where the curling waves o'er the wet sands creep,
And my heart responds to the sea's sad moan
  As all in vain for my love I weep.
O my dear, dead love! my only love,
  O love that I loved so fond and true,
Do you ever look down from your home above,
  Or think of the heart that is aching for you?

I remember well when you sailed away,
  We stood on the shore in the wind and rain,
And you said you'd come back to me, dear, some day,
  But ah! you will never come back again,
For under the cold, dark waves you sleep.
  Oh love, dear love my heart is sore,
And my eyes grow dim with the tears I weep
  For my dear, dead love, who will come no more.

With arms outstretched to the moaning sea
  I cry aloud in my dreary pain:
"Bring back the love that you stole from me,
  Oh! bring me my dear, lost love again,"
But the cold waves break on the grey sea shore
  And a sorrowful dirge they sing to me,
"You may weep and sigh till time is no more,
  But we'll never bring back thy love to thee."

And the dreary days drag wearily by,
  And I mourn and weep for the joys long past,
On leaden wings the moments fly,
  But the end must surely come at last.
O my dear, dead love, we will meet again
  On the golden shores of Eternity,
And my weary waiting will not be vain
  When the sea gives back what it stole from me.

Two Prayers.

A woman knelt in prayer and bowed her head,
And to her guardian angel softly said:
" O angel! tell me have the fates above
Decreed that I'll be blessed in my love?
I love so dearly and I fain would learn
If he I love doth love me in return."
The angel paused, then gently breathed a sigh
As in soft, pitying tones he made reply.
" Even as you love him so doth he love thee,
But Fate decrees that you must parted be."
She sighed, then murmured, " Still my life is blest,
If he but love me I can bear the rest."

Another woman prayed with drooping head:
" Oh Angel! will my love love me?" she said,
The Angel's tears fell fast like summer rain
As soft he answered her, " Thy prayer is vain;
He loves another and can never be
More than a true and faithful friend to thee,"
And then she slowly raised her drooping head
And smiling through her tears she softly said:
" He may not love me other than a friend,
But I love him and will unto the end
Of time, aye, and through all eternity
And that alone is heaven enough for me."

To E. S.

O heartstricken. sorrowing mother !
  No words ever written or said
Can lessen the weight of your sorrow
  Since the baby you love is dead.

But remember, O sorrowful mother
  Thy heart should rejoice, not repine.
Since of all earth's beautiful treasures
  The Master has chosen thine.

The fairest, the brightest, the purest,
  Find grace in His loving eyes
And the Lord hath chosen thy treasure
  To beautify Paradise.

Dear baby hands that will never
  Grow weary with earthly strife,
Sweet baby eyes that will never
  Grow dim with the cares of life.

Wee feet that will never stumble
  Over Life's rugged way,
For the hands of angels now guide them
  And they cannot go astray.

But a mother's love is boundless
  As the seas or the skies above,
And a mother's heart grows jealous
  E'en of the angels love.

And she longs for her baby's kisses,
  The touch of the dimpled hand,
And the baby voice now thrilling
  The ears of the angel band.

But you need not fear, O mother!
  Tho' the years be many or few,
Tho' the time pass slow or swiftly,
  For the baby heart is true.

Not even the songs of the angels
  Or the joys of Paradise
Can banish the tender yearning
  From your baby's gentle eyes

As she lingers beside the portal
  Of her shining, heavenly home
And asks of the angel warder
  If her mother soon will come.

And the wistful longing deepens
  In her eyes as she stands and waits,
Watching for mother darling
  At the City's pearly gates.

Cease then to mourn, sad mother,
  Take up Life's burden anew,
Shape thou the future before thee
  With earnest endeavor and true,

That no thought or deed unworthy
  May bring shame to the baby eyes
That are watching so wistfully for thee
  From the gates of Paradise.

Our Babies.

Willie and Annie, our two pretty babes,
  Our dear household angels, we love them so well;
Brown eyes and blue, so merry and glad,
  Which is the dearest, 'tis hard for to tell.
Dear little Nan with the nut-brown curls
  And bonnie brown eyes, so tender and true,
Willie with locks of the sunniest gold
  And eyes like a bit of Heaven's own blue.

When dear, little Willie climbs up on my knee,
  And gazes so lovingly into my face,
I think the wide world can hold nothing more dear
  Than our bonnie, wee lad, with his sweet baby
    ways.
While Nan with her tricks drives us all nearly wild,
  And we try, all in vain, to make her "be good,"
But I know as I clasp the sweet rogue to my heart,
  We would not have her otherwise e'en if we could.

O, innocent babies! so pure and so fair,
  You must soon wander forth in the world's busy
    strife,
And the dimpled, white hands will be wounded and
    torn,
  For thorns ever lurk 'neath the roses of life.
God guard you, and keep you, my innocent ones;
  May the sad tears of pain never dim your bright
    eyes.
The pathway before you seems cloudless and fair,
  God grant that no sorrow may darken the skies.

To M. A.

Even in the hour of her birth,
  When cradled on her mother's breast,
  A helpless babe, she lay at rest,
The angel Pain came down to earth.

And bending o'er the sleeping child,
  He laid a burden on her heart,
  Then turned, but e'er he could depart
The babe awoke and sweetly smiled.

The pathos in those great, dark eyes
  Went to his heart even as he spread
  His shining wings, then straight he sped
In silent swiftness to the skies.

And reaching Heaven the angel Pain
  Sought out the ranks of seraphs fair,
  And kissed the sweetest singer there,
Then winged his way to earth again.

And gazing on the child through tears,
  Upon her infant lips he left
  The kiss from heaven's singer reft,
A recompense for future years.

And as the maiden grew in years
  They marveled at her winsome grace,
  The sweetness of her voice and face,
Which moved mankind to smiles and tears.

But angels mourn while we rejoice
  To hear the strains, divine and sweet,
  For Heaven's choir is incomplete
Without the music of her voice.

The Lost Baby.

The birds are singing sweet and clear,
  Their songs are full of gladness,
The sun is shining bright, but still
  My heart is filled with sadness.

It matters not how glad the birds,
  Or fair the sunny day be.
My heart is heavy with its grief,
  I've lost my little baby.

Oh have you seen him passing by,
  A bonnie little fellow,
With eyes as blue as summer's sky
  And silky curls of yellow?

He disappeared quite suddenly
  And left no sign or token
To let me know where he has gone ;
  My heart is almost broken.

A manly lad is in his place,
  Much taller and much older,
With boots and pockets, sun-burned face,
  A school-bag on his shoulder.

Who clasps his arms around my neck,
  And laughs with boyish vigor—
" Why Auntie, dear, that baby's me,
  Only I'm grown up bigger. "

And did you really think me lost?
  How could you be so silly?
For though I'm grown up 'most a man
  I'm still your little Willy,

Who'll always love you just the same,
  And some day, Auntie, may be
You'll love me every bit as much
  As you have loved that baby."

Dear little man, a wistful note
  Into his voice is creeping,
Which warns me that the boyish heart
  Is full almost to weeping.

And so with tender words I haste
  To soothe his heart's dejection,
And strive with many a loving kiss
  To prove my fond affection.

Dear lad, I take you to my heart,
  To hold you there forever
And pray that stern misfortune's frown
  May rest upon you never.

But there's one chamber in my heart,
  Deep in the inmost center,
From all the rest it stands apart,
  Within it none may enter.

And there on Memory's golden shrine
  Is pictured bright and clearly,
The image of the baby boy
  I used to love so dearly.

Canada.

I love the land of Canada,
  The dear land of my birth ;
I deem my native country
  The fairest place on earth.
I love her lakes and rivers,
  Her forests, grand and high,
And her golden sunsets bright'ning
  The landscape to the eye.

I love the slender Tamarac,
  The tall and stately Pine,
The bonnie Birch and sturdy Oak
  With clinging Ivy vine.
So beautiful ! So glorious !
  In Autumn splendor drest,
I love them all, but ah ! I love
  The Maple Tree the best.

Old England has her Royal Rose,
  The Thistle's Scotland's pride,
Whilst many brave and gallant men
  For Erin's Shamrock died.
But give to me the Maple Leaf,
  More fair than all the rest,
Our country's precious emblem,
  The dearest and the best.

O lovely land of Canada
    May joy and peace be thine,
May the sun of bright prosperity
    O'er thy Dominion shine.
May thy sons be brave and noble,
    Thy daughters, true and kind,
And the love of home and country
    Our hearts in friendship bind.

Good Luck.

While passing through a meadow
    All wet with early dew,
I espied this four-leaved clover
    And gathered it for you.

They say a four-leaved clover
    Brings fortune, fair and true,
And so with loving wishes
    I send it, dear, to you.

Oh! May it bring you best of luck,
    And health and wealth galore ;
May all that's beautiful and bright
    For you be held in store.

May happiness be always thine,
    And peace your steps attend,
And Heaven's choicest blessings rest
    On you, my dearest friend.

The Bay of Quinte.

O lovely Bay of Quinte!
　Rolling on in tranquil flow,
Thine azure bosom tinted
　By the sunset's ruddy glow —
I might roam thro' every country,
　I might sail o'er every sea,
And never find a place more fair
　Than Quinte is to me.

No rugged cliffs nor mountains
　Outline thy tranquil shore,
But O the peaceful scenery !
　No heart could wish for more.
Thy sloping hills and valleys
　All clad in freshest green,
O fairer shores than Quinte's
　No mortal eye hath seen.

I love thee, Bay of Quinte!
　I love thy pleasant shores,
Thou art entwined with memories
　Of childhood's vanished hours.
Oft have I stood upon the shores
　Thy dancing wavelets kiss
And thought " 'Tis but in Heaven
　There are fairer scenes than this."

I love the Bay of Quinte,
　And when this life is o'er
And I with joyous steps will tread
　Dear Quinte's side no more,
Oh ! let me sleep by Quinte's side,
　More sweet would be my rest
Beside the pleasant waters
　I have always loved the best.

Just Like Me.

" Now Annie, be quiet." I sharply say,
" I have had enough of your noise to-day,
And I think it is time you tried to be good,
And behave yourself as a little girl should.
Why do you persist in acting so?
You're the naughtiest little girl I know."

I pause, and Nan looks demurely down
To hide the gleam in her eyes so brown,
Then says : " Dear Auntie, I s'pose it's so,
I am very naughty, but then you know
Grandma says that you used to be,
When you were a little girl, just like me.

" She says you played ' hookey ' 'most every day
With Uncle Eddie down to the Bay,
And you two used to fight like cats and dogs,
And push one another off the logs
In the shallow water, just for fun,
Then sit on the logs and dry in the sun.
And you used to run the big boom 'round,
And once you fell in and were nearly drowned,
But some men heard Uncle Eddie shout
And came just in time to pull you out.

" And you used to dress and nurse the cat,
And play in the sun without any hat,
'Till she'd think your very brains would bake,
And you ' hooked ' her pies and ' fobbled ' her cake.
And often you and my Uncle Ed
For being naughty were sent to bed,
Without any supper, and you used to cry
When you had to wash dishes, same as I.

" And you used to run off to the fields for flowers,
And stay away for hours and hours,
Then slip in the back way upstairs to bed,
You and Aunt Emmie and Uncle Ed.
And she says you could climb a fence or tree,
And tear your clothes just the same as me.

" So, Auntie. I think it is hardly fair."
The dear little maid goes on to declare,
" That you should be always scolding so
Because I am naughty, when you know
You did the very same things I do.
So Grandma says, and it must be true."

Like a culprit I sit and listen, dismayed,
To the charges read by this little maid,
I am vanquished, ay ! But I bear no grudge
As I plead my guilt to the youthful judge,
For memory wakes with a rush and whirl,
Aroused by the words of the little girl,
And, looking down in the bright, young face
The well-known features and smile I trace
Of another wee lassie I used to know
Somewhere about twenty years ago.

And I close my eyes while memory strays
Back to my wild, sweet childhood's days,
And my heart beats fast and my pulses stir
As I think of **when I was** "**just** like her."

'Then two dimpled arms around me twine
As the honest brown eyes glance **into mine**,
Meeting **my gaze** so fearlessly
As this strange question she puts to me,
A question that thrills me through and through,
" **When I** grow up **will I** be like you ?

For I think " she goes on in a musing tone,
" It is awfully jolly to live alone,
Without any husband to grumble and growl,
Or bothersome babies to fret and howl,
But just a dear, little niece like me,"
How the brown eyes sparkle with mischievous glee !
" To come now and then to visit you
And make things lively, same as I do.
And when called ' old maid ' by people unkind,
To smile so serene, as if you don't mind.
O, I think it's so nice to be big and wise
And have dear, little wrinkles around your eyes,
And write nice verses and stories too.
Oh ! I'd love to grow up and be just like you."

" Just like me." Ah ! She does not think
How her prattle causes my heart to sink,
As memory kneels o'er the grave of the Past,
While the blinding tears fall thick and fast,
Weaving a shadowy veil between
My longing eyes and what might have been.

" Just like me." Forbid, O God !
She should ever look back over pathways trod,
As I have done, and see through tears,
The shattered hopes and dreams of years.
Grant that her lips may never quaff,
As mine have done, Pain's bitter draught.
Father ! I pray, may it so Thee please
That all resemblance between us cease,
And her life no more be likened to mine
When once she has crossed the boundary line
That divides the battle-field of Life
From the gardens with childish pleasures rife.
" Just like me." Forbid, O God
That her feet should tread where mine have trod.

Then smiling down in the clear, brown eyes
That have watched my emotion with grave surprise,
I clasp her close as I pray that she
May never grow up to be "just like me."

Her Answer.

They said to her, " Why are your songs so sad?
  Such hidden pain and pathos in them lie,
Such mournful thoughts in sombre language clad,
  They bring the tears unbidden to the eye.
If you would only sing in strains more glad
  The world would laugh, and so forget to sigh.

" Life has its pain, but has its pleasures too !
  A cheery smile is better than a tear ;
Some hearts are false, we know, but some are true,
  The world is sad, why make it still more drear ?
We love Life's roses better than Life's rue,
  Better than dirge of woe the song of cheer."

And as they talked with her in cheerful strain
  A shadow stole o'er her averted face,
But when she turned to meet their gaze again
  Her smiling lips showed naught of sorrow's trace,
Though in her eyes still lurked a shade of pain
  Which naught might banish from its dwelling place.

The lark sings gaily in the morning sun
  Uprising from its nest amid the wheat;
The nightingale's sweet notes, when day is done,
  Float gently from the woodland's cool retreat
In soft and plaintive strains, yet is there one
  Who hearing both, would deem the lark's more sweet ?

" A smile is better than a tear you say,
  Believe me, friends, it is not always so,
As I can prove. 'Twas but the other day
  I stood with one whose heart was crushed with woe,
Beside the coffin where her treasure lay,
  So great, so deep her grief, tears would not flow.

" Upon my breast she laid her aching head,
  I tried to comfort her, but words were vain,
But as my tears fell fast above the dead
  Her tears burst forth in showers like the rain;
Then when her grief was spent, she smiled and said:
  ' Dear friend, those tears have eased my heart's dull
    pain.'"

Soul and Mind.

H ere at the glass I stand and wait
  To meet that cold, proud gaze of thine,
Some questions I would put to thee,
  So answer true, O Soul of mine!

Lift up those clear, calm eyes to mine,
  Calm eyes that search me thro' and thro',
And listen while I question thee,
  O Soul of mine and answer true.

Life is so full of mysteries
  That are not understood by men.
So full of problems yet unsolved,
  Too deep and vast for human ken.

Mine eyes, earth-blinded, vainly strive
  To read each wondrous mystery,
But thou art heaven-born, they say,
  O Soul! It must be plain to thee.

Then tell me, was it worth my while
  To live thro' all those dull, gray years,
With scarce a ray of joy or light
  To lift the clouds of grief and tears.

When as a child I knew no wrong,
  And hope within my heart beat high,
When faith in human kind was strong,
  O Soul! Were it not best to die?

When Love's sweet magic thrilled my soul,
　And Life a paradise did seem,
O Soul! Were it not best to die
　Than live to find it all a dream?

And when I tried to reach the goal
　Upon the heights so far above,
Another passed me in the race
　And won the prize for which I strove.

And as I watched my fair hopes die,
　My heart grew cold and hard as stone.
Then balked Ambition vanquished Faith,
　Whilst cruel Doubt usurped her throne.

O Soul! Thou knowest how I tried
　To keep my faith in God and man,
But every hope was swept from me.
　Why was it?　Answer, if you can.

Soul! Is there joy enough in Heaven
　To make amends for human woe?
Can all eternity atone
　For what we suffer here below!

The preacher bids us kiss the rod,
　And bow our heads to Heaven's decree,
Says Sorrow is the lot of man ;
　But tell me, Soul! Why must it be?

Nay, gaze not with accusing eyes,
　Mine eyes can stare as well as thine,
Those questions I have put to thee,
　Thou can'st not answer, Soul of mine!

＊　　＊　　＊　　＊　　＊　　＊　　＊　　＊　　＊　　＊

A clear, sweet voice stole on **my** ear,
　A voice of wondrous melody,
As from the **mirror's** crystal depths
　My Soul looked out and answered me.

I cannot tell you what she **said,**
　For words of mine are all too **weak ;**
It was no language of this earth
　In which my Soul to me did **speak.**

Oh ! Wondrous were the words she spake,
　Wisdom and Truth, sublime and grand !
They hushed my mind's wild questioning
　And fell upon my heart like balm.

Her eyes met mine with steadfast gaze,
　Until, abashed, I gazed no more,
But knelt before my God, and prayed
　As I had never prayed before.

From Out the Depths.

The night is closing fast around me, Lord,
  The shades of darkness gather, swift and gray,
My aching eyes can scarcely pierce the gloom,
  And my weak, faltering feet have lost the **way**,
O come to me in Sorrow's dreary night
And lead me from the darkness into light.

There was a time when I was well content
  To walk within the paths appointed me,
But listening to my heart's rebellious voice
  I wandered, step by step, afar from Thee.
Night cometh fast, and swiftly fades the day ;
  Father have pity, I have lost my way.

When, hand in hand, I walked with Thee, dear Lord,
  Thy strength upheld me in my darkest hour,
But now my burden bends me to the earth—
  I miss the aid of Thy sustaining power.
Lord, turn from me the vengeance of Thy wrath
  And lead my faltering steps along the path.

My sin is this, O Lord, I tried to solve
  Those problems that are known to none but Thee.
Bewildered and perplexed, I vainly strove
  To find an answer to Life's mystery.
Thus, step by step, the dangerous path I trod
  Till like the fool, I said : "There is no God."

Lord, I confess with tears, my sin is great,
  But, penitent and humbled in the dust,
I ask Thy pardon for my waywardness ;
  Have pity on me, Lord, in Thee I trust,
Hear Thou my cry of penitence and grief :
  "Lord ! I believe, help Thou my unbelief."

The Lesson.

Once when my heart had dared to spurn
  The wisdom of His will sublime,
God set a task for me to learn—
  To break this stubborn will of mine.

Humbled and penitent, I knelt
  At my stern teacher Sorrow's knee,
And with white lips, heart-stricken spelt
  The lesson God had set for me.

Through shades of swiftly gathering night
  I strove the tear-stained page to con,
Whilst friends who smiled with morning's light
  Departed as the night came on.

Then with my lesson learned by heart
  I turned to face the world again,
And watched each fickle friend depart,
  Mine eyes bedimmed with tears of pain.

I scanned each face with wistful eyes
  For friendly smile, but there was none,
Then turned away with bitter sigh
  And cried: "O God! There is not one,

"Who heedless of the world's cold scorn
  Will step from out the beaten road,
And help with words of kindness born
  A comrade sinking 'neath the load."

O friend! I own that I was wrong,
  My hasty judgment now I rue,
You stepped from out that worldly throng
  To clasp my hand in friendship true.

The memory of that kindly deed
  Shall ever in my heart be shrined,
For in that hour of sorest need
  You saved my faith in human kind.

And though God's hand hath smitten sore,
  Hath broken this poor heart of mine,
And darkened all that lies before,
  I will not murmur nor repine.

For had my sun ne'er known eclipse,
  Had Life's fair blooms ne'er turned to rue,
Had Sorrow's cup not pressed my lips,
  I had not found a friend like you.

Of all I know, 'twas you alone,
  Who stretched towards me helping hands,
Content to let the fruitless past
  Be judged by Him who understands.

Your hand had power my steps to stay
  As unbelief's dark paths I trod,
And pointed out a better way,
  The peaceful path that leads to God.

Unanswered Prayers.

I asked for Love, God would not grant my **prayer**;
　I prayed for Fame, and still He said me nay;
I could not understand His loving care,
　That what He did was **for** my good alway.

And so I murmured at the stern decree,
　Rebellious anger swelling **in my** breast;
He smiled forgiveness **as** He said to me:
　"**My child,** all that I do is **for** the best."

And now my heart is cold to Love's sweet voice;
　Ambition's flame lies lifeless in my breast;
Nor Love, nor Fame can make my heart rejoice—
　The only boon I ask of God is Rest.

My prayer is yet unanswered, but I know
　That God knows best how much my heart can bear;
When it hath borne the allotted share of woe
　I know that he will hearken to my prayer.

His time and justice I can safely bide
　Knowing that He will grant me this request,
And all Life's longings will be satisfied
　In that sweet hour when God will give me Rest.

Your Sunny Smile.

In summer when the skies were blue
    And sunshine bathed the land with light,
When friends were mine whom I deemed true
    And Life seemed pleasant to my sight,
With sunny smile you came to me
    And promised love and fealty.

Fairer than sunbeams did appear
    The sunshine of your smile to me,
The love-light in your eyes more clear
    Than all the light on land and sea,
And all my heart went out to you—
I loved you and believed you true.

The sun withdrew, and all the land
    Grew dark, the world spoke harsh of me,
Friends fell away on every hand,
    I mourned them not, I still had thee ;
But when I sought you in my need
    Your love proved but a broken reed.

'Twas but a cloud, and soon it passed,
    The sun shone fairer than before ;
Old friends returned, even you at last
    Smiled on me as in days of yore,
But I had learned in that dark while
    To live without your sunny smile.

My Friend.

I had no friend! With heavy burdened heart
  And drooping head, alone I walked through Life
And in the world's gay pleasures had no part ;
  My soul was wearied with the bitter strife.
Unloved, unknown, I wandered through Life's mart,
  Through gloomy paths with many a sorrow rife.
                    I had no friend.

The skies o'er head were heavy, dull and gray,
  Without one ray of sunshine breaking through,
My starving heart grew faint along the way,
  When glancing up I met your gaze so true,
Then all the dreary night was changed to day
  And I rejoiced, dear heart, because I knew
                    I'd found a friend.

You never failed me, loving friend and true,
  Since that glad hour when we two first did meet,
No longer do I dread Life's bitter rue
  Which Friendship's lips have touched and rendered
    sweet,
Still rough the paths that I must journey through,
  But what care I tho' tempests 'round me beat,
                    I have a friend.

The Coming of the King.

O God ! Dost Thou not hear the bitter wailing
    Ascending from the Earth unto Thy Throne?
Are human tears and prayers so unavailing
    That Heaven heareth not our sobbing moan ?

" As a shepherd feeds his flock," so it is written,
    Lord, we believe, even as Thou hast said,
Yet see, O God ! By Famine's gaunt hand smitten
    Thy children faint and die, They have no bread.

Thou hast endowed the Earth with goodly treasure
    That each may have a portion, fair and just,
And bade Thy stewards give with flowing measure,
    Yet see, O Lord, how they abuse Thy Trust.

Hearken, O God ! O King, in justice hearken !
    Earth's toiling millions moan in agony,
How long, dear God, must man's oppression darken
    The lives of those who put their trust in Thee ?

O Angel host, whose songs are ever ringing
    Around Jehovah's Throne, so sweet and clear,
For one brief moment cease, O cease thy singing,
    And let Earth's bitter wailing reach His ear.

Weep on, ye sufferers, raise your moans to Heaven,
  Let cries of anguish swell more loud and long
Until Earth's pain the jasper walls hath riven,
  And hushed the rapture of the angels' song.

———

There was silence in Heaven around the Throne,
As up from the Earth came a sobbing moan
Fraught with such anguish and bitter wrong
That the singers in Heaven hushed their song,
And the Lord stooped down from His Throne to hear
Earth's bitter cry as it reached His ear,
And His heart was moved for the woes of men—
" My children need me on Earth again."
Then He said to His shining herald : " Go,
Wing thy swift way to the world below,
And proclaim this message unto all men,
' The King is coming to Earth again.'"

Through the Gates of Pearl, like a winged flame,
Down to the Earth the Angel came,
And the hearts of men, erstwhile so sad
With the cares of Life, grew light and glad
When they heard the tidings the herald bore :
" Rejoice ! The King is coming once more."
And all the rulers met to plan
How Earth should welcome the Son of Man.

And they summoned the myriad slaves of Earth,
The sad-faced toilers of humble birth,
Saying: " Work ! We bid ye, O slaves of the land !
Build us a mansion, more high and grand

Than ever was seen on Earth before,
For our King is coming to rule once more,
So build us a palace, grand and great,
Where our King can rule in royal state."

And the toilers labored with all their might
Through many a weary day and night,
And the palace walls rose high and grand
'Neath the wondrous skill of brain and hand,
And the feast was spread in the banquet hall
Where the rich and mighty assembled all,
And luxury, warmth and light were there,
And the glimmer and gleam of jewels rare,
In costliest garments all were dressed
Waiting to welcome the Kingly Guest,
And the sheen of garments, rich and grand,
The labor of woman's toil-worn hands,
And the bells rang out in joyous mirth
To welcome the Prince of Peace to Earth.

And the work of the weary slaves was o'er.
Their masters needed their toil no more;
All was in readiness for the guest,
And the weary slaves, for a while might rest.
" Hasten," they said, "'from the palace door,
All ye who are lowly-born and poor.
When the King arrives in royal state
It is fitting that none but the rich and great,
The ruler, the statesman, the scribe and priest,
Should sit with Him at the royal feast;
So depart, ye slaves, from the palace door,
Go, seek your homes in the haunts of the poor,
Lest your garments worn and your faces thin
Should offend His eyes as He enters in."

And the weary toilers went slowly home
Through the darkening streets.   Their work was done.
But some of them lingered and dared to stay
To see the King as He passed that way,
Though the royal feast was not for them,
Yet **they** all might touch His garment's hem.

But even as the rulers sat in state,
A knock was heard at the palace gate,
" The King has come at last," they cried,
And their hearts beat fast with joy and pride,
" Our King has kept His royal word,
Let us all go forth to meet our Lord."
And they all went forth, that stately **throng,**
And the palace gates were open flung,
And there in the entrance stood a man
In the humble garb of **an artizan.**

A murmur of anger, loud and long,
Went up from that jeweled, silk-robed throng,
That one from the ranks of the low and **poor**
Should dare to knock at the palace door ;
And they frowned on him as he meekly said :
" **I am** tired and hungry, give me bread,
I have journeyed many a mile this day,
And my path lay over a rugged way,
My limbs are weary and ready to sink,
I am tired and thirsty, **give me** drink."

But they answered him **as with one accord,**
" This is the palace of Christ the Lord ;
Within the hall the feast is spread.
Is it right that a beggar should eat the bread

That is meant for a Prince of Royal Race?"
And they shut the door in the stranger's face.

Then they all went back to the banquet room,
And they waited long for the King to come;
And the lights burned dim as the night wore on,
And hope from their bosoms was almost gone,
And they said at the first, faint gleam of day:
" Surely the King has lost His way.
Let us go forth with willing feet
Through every by-way and every street ;
Let us hasten before it is too late,
And show Him the way to the palace gate."

So all that day, with willing feet
They searched through the crowded city street
For a Kingly Stranger, but all in vain ;
And their tears fell fast like the summer rain
And their sorrow was deep as well as loud,
For they loved their King, but their hearts were proud.

They found Him when day was almost o'er,
'Mid the humble homes of the toiling poor.
With a worshiping crowd around Him pressed,
In glad amaze, He had stripped His breast
Of the royal mantle, and wrapped it 'round
A shivering outcast of the town,
Whilst closely clasped to His sheltering breast
A baby slumbered in peaceful rest—
A poor little babe, a child of sin,
With the brand of shame on its features thin,
Whilst the jeweled crown that had graced His head
He had given the poor, to sell for bread.

Then pushing the humble throng aside
The rulers knelt at His feet and cried :
" O King ! We have sought Thee long in vain,
And our **hearts** were heavy with grief and pain ;
Come, **let us bring** Thee **to** the gates
Of Thy **royal hall, where** the feast awaits."

Christ looked at them with meek, sad eyes,
And they all shrank back in shamed surprise ;
They had seen that look of patient grace
When **they** shut the door **in the** stranger's face.
" **Ye** knew **Me not,** and denied Me bread,
When I knocked at the door last night," He said.

Rest.

"I am so tired," a weary woman said,
And on her pillow laid her aching head;
I have been toiling hard through all the day,
Dear Lord, I am so tired I cannot pray,
My brain is throbbing, and my eyes are dim,
And all my tired senses seem to swim;
Since Life holds naught for me but toil and pain,
Would I might sleep and never wake again."
And as she on her pillow lay and wept
Sweet sleep descended on her and she slept.

And in the silent hour of midnight gloom
An angel softly stole into the room,
And gliding noiselessly unto the bed,
Laid its light hand upon the sleeper's head.
The woman woke and marveled at the sight,
For all the room was filled with radiant light.
Then, as the angel bent and kissed her brow,
She murmured softly, "Tell me who art thou?"
Then as the angel clasped her to its breast
She cried: "I know thee now, thy name is Rest."

And in the morn they came and found her there,
Her pale, worn features rendered calm and fair,
Beneath the wondrous majesty of Death,
And as they gazed on her with bated breath,
They marveled at the beauty and the grace
That rested on the sleeper's peaceful face.
And then they robed her form in garments fair,
And from her brow they brushed the soft, brown hair,
And crossed her toil-worn hands upon her breast
And so she slept in sweet, eternal rest.

Only a Working Girl.

I know I am only a working girl,
　And I am not ashamed to say
I belong to the ranks of those who toil
　For a living, day by day.
With willing feet I press along
　In the paths that I must tread,
Proud that I have the strength and skill
　To earn my daily bread.

I belong to the "lower classes ; "
　That's a phrase we often meet.
There are some who sneer at working girls ;
　As they pass us on the street,
They stare at us in proud disdain
　And their lips in scorn will curl,
And oftentimes we hear them say :
　" She's only a working girl."

" Only a working girl ! " Thank God,
　With willing hands and heart,
Able to earn my daily bread,
　And in Life's battle take my part.
You could offer me no title
　I would be more proud to own,
And I stand as high in the sight of God
　As the Queen upon her throne.

Those gentle folk who pride themselves
　Upon their wealth and birth,
And look with scorn on those who have
　Naught else but honest worth,
Your gentle birth we laugh to scorn,
　For we hold it as our creed
That none are gentle, save the one
　Who does a gentle deed.

We are only the "lower classes,"
　But the Holy Scriptures tell
How, when the King of Glory
　Came down on earth to dwell,
Not with the rich and mighty
　'Neath costly palace dome,
But with the poor and lowly
　He chose to make His home.

He was one of the "lower classes,"
　And had to toil for bread,
So poor that oftentimes He had
　No place to lay His head.
He knows what it is to labor
　And toil the long day thro',
He knows when we are weary
　For He's been weary too.

O working girls! Remember,
　It is neither crime or shame
To work for honest wages,
　Since Christ has done the same,
And wealth and high position
　Seem but of little worth
To us, whose fellow laborer
　Is King of Heaven and Earth.

So when you meet with scornful sneers,
　Just lift your heads in pride ;
The shield of honest womanhood
　Can turn such sneers aside,
And some day they will realize
　That the purest, fairest pearls
'Mid the gems of noble womankind
　Are "only working girls."

The Honest Working Man.

As through the world we take our way
  How oftentimes we hear
The praises sung of wealthy men,
  Of prince, and duke and peer.
The poets tell us of their fame,
  They are lauded o'er the land,
But you very seldom hear them sing
  Of the honest working man.

They praise the wealthy banker,
  The purse-proud millionaire ;
Their pockets have golden lining,
  So they're praised from everywhere.
Let others sing the praises
  Of those darlings of the land,
But mine shall be a nobler theme—
  The honest working man.

Let monarchs prize their glittering crowns
  And all their royal host,
Let lordlings brag of their blue blood—
  They have nothing else to boast.
But what is all their rank, compared
  To our hero, true and grand,
One of fair Nature's noblemen—
  The honest working man.

His hands may be both rough and hard,
　His clothes and speech be plain,
But you will find his manly heart
　Without a spot or stain.
And there are some whose clothes are fine,
　Whose hands are soft and white,
But the secret records of their lives
　Could never bear the light.

May Heaven's choicest blessings fall
　Upon that hero's head,
Who bravely toils throughout each day
　To earn his loved ones bread.
You'll find no monarch who can show
　A record half so grand.
God bless great labor's true-born knight—
　The honest working man.

So now of Fortune's favored ones,
　Henceforth let less be said,
And more be spoken of the man
　Who toils for daily bread.
God bless each hardy son of toil
　That labors in the land.
Let us give three cheers with right good will
　For the honest working man.

Lend a Hand.

Life is full of hidden perils,
   And the traveller never thinks
Of the dangers that surround him,
   Till the ground beneath him sinks.
Can you calmly stand and watch him
   Sinking in the treacherous sand,
Heeding not his cry of anguish?
   Shame upon you! Lend a hand!

When you see a young beginner
   Struggling up the steps of Fame,
And in spite of opposition
   Striving hard to win a name,
You who've gained the heights before him
   And upon the summit stand,
Do not idly watch his struggles,
   Rouse yourselves and lend a hand.

When you see a wounded brother
   On the battle-field of Life,
Who, after fighting, long and nobly,
   Falls, a loser in the strife,
Pause one moment, O ye conquerors,
   In your rush to victory grand,
Brave as ye he fought, tho' vainly.
   He is wounded. Lend a hand!

When you meet a fallen sister
  In the crowded city street,
None to give her kindly counsel,
  None to guide her wayward feet—
In God's eyes she's just as precious
  As the purest in the land.
Speak no word of scorn or censure,
  Try to save her. Lend a hand !

And perhaps, in that dread hour
  When all secrets are made known,
When at last both saint and sinner
  Stand before the Judgment Throne,
When in answer to the summons,
  At the Bar of God you stand,
Waiting for the eternal sentence,
  You'll be glad you lent a hand.

Two Poets.

There lived a poet once, a famous bard,
　Whose muse, arrayed in robes of misty light,
Soared high above the common herd of men.
　So high she soared, she almost passed from sight,
Even as the cold and brilliant stars of Heaven
　That shine in chilly splendour from the skies
Withhold the radiance of their fairest beams
　Beyond the naked sight of human eyes.
Still there are some pretentious ones who read
　The mystic dreams and fancies of his brain,
Pedantic minds, who, understanding naught,
　Would still have others think they grasp the strain,
Till, at some passage with strange meaning fraught,
　Too subtle far for them to understand,
They pause perplexed, then as with one accord
　Cry out in chorus: " How sublime and grand ! "
O gifted bard ! I would not try to pluck
　One leaf from out thy laurel wreath of fame
Because I fail to grasp thy subtle thought ;
　'Tis not in thee, but me, where lies the blame.
Around his tomb the world has bowed in grief,
　And strewed his grave with bay and laurel leaf.

There lived and died a poet, years ago—
　A hardy, humble ploughman of the soil
Who sang his heartfelt songs in simplest words
　And earned his daily bread by humble toil.

His songs brought gladness unto many hearts
  And soothed men's sorrows as with magic spell.
His name was known in palace and in cot,
  For king and peasant loved the poet well.
And why?   Because he sang of human faith,
  Of human love, of human joy and pain,
The grandest thoughts couched in the simplest words,
  The lowliest mind could grasp the meaning plain.
O poet ploughmen! thine the laurel wreath,
  Whose songs found answer in the hearts of men,
Thy name shall live on Fame's immortal scroll
  After his name has passed from mortal ken,
Thine the true poet soul and master mind
  Whose lyrics touched the hearts of all mankind.

In Memoriam, G. P. Y.

Just three-score years and ten he spent with us,
The span of Life allotted unto man,
And then before old age had dimmed his eye
Or clouded his great intellect and brain,
God's voice spake out to him and called him hence.
And he obeyed the call, nor shrank when Death,
That grim and ghastly King of Terrors, laid
His hand upon his noble heart, and stilled
Its kindly throbs.   No coward sign he made,
But undismayed and fearless, he went forth
Into the great, mysterious unknown,
Whose entrance is the Grave, whose password—Death.

And now to him all secrets are revealed ;
Those mysteries, unfathomed and profound,
Those problems which we ever try to solve
With all the might of our poor human ken—
Problems which baffled even his great brain—
Are all unfolded now unto his sight
Like printed pages of an open book.
Ah ! If he only could come back again
For one brief space of time, and speak to us
Of those great mysteries, profound and vast,
Which are no longer mysteries to him.
But that can never be, such thoughts are vain,
For our earth-blinded eyes must e'en as his

Be touched and opened by the hand of Death,
Ere we can hope to read the truths sublime
Inscribed within the pages of that book.

And we who know how quenchless was his thirst
For Truth and Knowledge, though we mourn our loss,
Rejoice to picture him in that far land,
Drinking deep draughts of knowledge from the springs
Of glorious, eternal, living Truth.
And knowing this we would not wish thee back,
Teacher and guide, philosopher and sage,
Who lived as God ordained mankind should live,
Who died as God ordained mankind should die,
Whose life was blameless and whose end was peace.

A New Year's Greeting.

Long years have passed since we **last met,**
    Long years of mingled joy and pain,
And years may come and vanish yet
                Ere we two meet again.

The path I've trod since then, dear friend,
    Has proven rough unto my feet :
I've learned that Life holds in the end
                More bitterness than sweet.

And now on this glad New **Year's day,**
    When all the land is bright with **cheer,**
I pause beside the mile-stone gray
                That marks another **year.**

Here Friendship comes with outstretched **hand**
    Her chosen, favored ones to meet.
Unnoticed and alone I stand—
                I have no friend to **greet.**

In bitterness I turn away
    And sigh : " Is there **not one that's** true,
Whose friendship can **outlast a day ? "**
                And **then I think** of you.

O truest heart ! O noblest friend
    God ever sent to comfort me,
Here at the Old Year's fruitless end
                My soul cries out to thee.

Across the gulf of weary years
  My lonely spirit calls to thine,
And memory brings the sudden tears,
         My friend of " Auld Lang Syne."

How shall I word the message, dear,
  My greeting for this New Year's day?
How write the words of kindly cheer
         That my full heart would say?

May all your life from care be free,
  Not crushed as mine, 'neath Sorrow's thrall,
The sunlight God denied to **me**
         Across your pathway fall.

Death of the Old Year.

In the silent hour of midnight
  Like a mystic phantom gray,
Head bowed low in weeping **sorrow,**
  So the Old Year steals away.
None bestow a thought upon him,
  For his death none shed a tear,
All are thinking of **the** morrow,
  Of the blithe and bright New **Year.**

Hastening on **with** weary footsteps,
  Wailing oft in saddened tone :
" No one cares for **all** my sorrow,
  No one grieves that I am gone."
Shivering in the bitter night **wind,**
  Death's dark shadows looming **near,**
By every one he is deserted.
  Poor, forsaken, sad Old Year !

Now the midnight chimes are telling
  Of the gladsome **New** Year's birth ;
How their **cheery tones** are swelling
  Into joyous songs of mirth
Whilst in bitter, lonely sorrow,
  Passing on through pathways drear,
To the sea of **dark** Oblivion,
  Glides the lonely, **sad** Old Year.

Christmas Memories.

Christmas bells are softly pealing
  Through the frosty morning air,
O'er my heart the notes are stealing,
  Driving out the pain and care.
Clearer now their tones are ringing
  Over the new-fallen snow,
Once again the tidings bringing,
  Brought by angels long ago.

And my thoughts are softly turning
  To a vanished Christmas day,
And my heart is filled with yearning
  For the dear ones far away,
Sad, sweet memories, swiftly thronging
  Thrill my breast with joy and pain,
And I long with tender longing
  To be with them once again,

O! the time seems long and dreary
  Since those parting words were said,
And the path is rough and weary
  That my tired feet must tread.
Yet though my life is filled with sadness,
  Still with fervent heart I pray,
May their lives be filled with gladness
  And peace be theirs this Christmas day.

The New Year.

When the gloomy shades of midnight
  Have enveloped all the earth,
I sit watching at the window
  For the coming New Year's birth,
And I seem to see in fancy,
  Through the shadows of the night,
Hosts of angel forms advancing,
  O so fair and wondrous bright.

Well I know those radiant beings
  Are not of an earthly clime—
In their midst a grim old figure,
  Gaunt and gray, old Father Time ;
In his arms he bears a burden—
  'Tis an infant, young and fair,
Rounded limbs and baby dimples,
  Laughing eyes and shining hair.

Onward comes the bright procession,
  Singing songs of happy cheer,
And I know the smiling infant
  Is the blithe and bright New Year.
Now they pause before my window
  And the New Year laughs with glee,
Holding both hands clasped tightly
  O'er the gifts I may not see.

And he whispers : " O sad mortal !
  Bid thy sorrows all depart,
I have come with fairest blessings
  And would cheer thy saddened heart."
And I whisper : " Tell me, New Year,
  What thou hast in store for me ? "
But he clasps his hand still closer
  O'er the gifts I may not see.

And he speaks in solemn sadness
  " Mortal, would'st thou look ahead,
Would'st thou draw aside the curtain
  From the paths that thou must tread ?
Never yet were seen by mortals,
  Paths as yet by them untrod,
Seek not then to read the future,
  Leave it all to time and God."

Then with footsteps fleet and noiseless,
  Speed the shining throng away
And once more alone I'm sitting
  In the darkness, cold and gray.
" Ah ! The New Year's right," I murmur,
  " It is best I should not know,
So to God I leave the future
  Be it weal or be it woe."

A Christmas Prayer.

Dear Lord, at this glad Christmas tide,
　　When loving friends with joyous mirth
Meet 'round each cheerful Christmas hearth,
　　Is there no Christmas guest for me?
See Lord, my heart's door opened wide,
　　O, enter Thou, with me abide ;
This anniversary of Thy birth
　　Wilt Thou not deign my guest to be?

Lord, when with loving hearts aglow,
　　Friend greeteth friend with Christmas cheer,
They offer gifts through friendship dear,
　　Hast Thou no Christmas gift for me?
Dear Lord, to me Thy kindness show,
　　I long so much Thy Peace to know,
Come Thou unto my hearth-stone drear
　　And bring the gift of Peace with Thee.

The Dying Year.

The New Year comes to me with laughing eyes,
  His hands clasped closely that I may not see,
And whispers of the wondrous gifts he holds
  Safe hidden in his dimpled palms for me.
But all his promises to me are naught,
  His words but fall upon a heedless ear.
To all his glowing hopes I give no thought
  For I am weeping for the dying year.

Oh! Dear Old Year, and must I say farewell?
  Never indeed was word so sadly said.
I care not for the New Year's promises,
  With thee my fairest hopes will soon be dead.
Old Year, thou wast indeed a friend to me
  And though my joy were sometimes mixed with woe
No other year was half so kind as thee;
  It breaks my heart, Old Year, to see thee go.

Hark! Now the bells ring out their merry chime!
  Upon the midnight air their voices swell
A peal of welcome to the new-born year.
  To me 'tis but the Old Year's dying knell.
O, dear old friend, the hour has come at last
  When I must say farewell for aye to thee.
New Years may come and Old Years pass away,
  But you will never be forgot by me.

St. Valentine's Eve.

" Good St. Valentine, listen to me,
Good St. Valentine, let me see
Who my future love will be ? "
—Old Rhyme.

I was all alone at the window
  On the eve of St. Valentine's day,
And the moon shed a soft, silver lustre,
  O'er the earth clad in snowy array.

And I hope, dear, you'll not think me foolish
  When you hear what I have to tell,
But sitting alone in the moonlight
  · I thought of the old love-spell.

They say if you stand in the moonlight
  And pray to St. Valentine
For a glimpse of your future lover
  In the words of a quaint, old rhyme,

That the good Saint never refuses
  To answer a prayer sincere,
And the form of the one who loves you
  That night in your dreams will appear.

So I thought if he listened to others
  He might answer a prayer of mine,
For you know he's the friend of lovers,
  This dear old Saint Valentine.

But I fear I'm a bit of sceptic
   For I hadn't much faith in the charm,
Still I thought to myself,"" I will try it,
   As it surely can do no harm."

And the moon shed its glories around me
   As I whispered the quaint old rhyme,
And of course, dear, I need not tell you
   I was thinking of you all the time.

Oh ! I whispered it ever so softly
   For fear I might be overheard,
But the moon and the stars seemed to listen
   And I know that they caught every word.

And I fancied the moon was smiling
   And the stars seemed to laugh overhead,
And I felt half ashamed of my folly
   As I silently crept to my bed.

But, dear, I awoke in the morning
   Convinced that the charm was true,
And I know that the good Saint heard me,
   For, darling, I dreamed of you.

Hallowe'en.

As I sit alone by the fire
  This quiet Hallowe'en,
My heart revives with the memory
  Of a past and happy scene,
How their forms arise before me,
  The dear friends of the past,
But how soon the visions vanish,
  Too bright by far to last!

I seem to feel their presence
  In the swiftly gathering gloom,
And I hear their garments rustle
  In the stillness of the room,
And gentle mem'ry rolls away
  The years that intervene
Between me and the pleasure
  Of that happy Hallowe'en.

A merry, laughing party,
  With lips and eyes aglow,
With ringing laugh and merry jest—
  What thought had we of woe?
O loved ones dear, since that glad night,
  Sad years have come and gone,
And of all the bright and happy group,
  I am sitting here alone.

Alone of all that happy group;
  Some sleep beneath the ground,
And winter winds sweep o'er their **graves**
  With sad and mournful sound.
And some by happy firesides,
  With children, bright and fair,
Encircled by Love's shelt'ring arms
  They know **no pain nor care.**

And one, ah me, the dearest one
  Of all that household band,
Has drained the cup of sorrow
  From Fate's relentless hand.
Better, dear heart, if thou **had'st died**
  In childhood, long ago,
Than live to see thy future **marred**
  By memories of woe.

And as I sit here dreaming,
  It seems so long ago,
Like a day of brightest sunshine
  Veiled by weary years of woe,
And I bow my head in sorrow
  While my soul cries out in pain ;
Will those days of peace and **gladness**
  Ne'er come to us again ?

Then a voice of silvery music
  Comes stealing through the room,
And a presence, sweet and mystic,
  Seems to lighten up the gloom,
It lulls my bitter yearnings
  Into calm and peaceful rest,
As it bids me not to murmur
  For God knows what is best.

It is the lot of mortals
  To feel the weight of woe.
If we would wear the crown in heaven
  We must bear the cross below.
I know some day we all will meet
  Where Sorrow cannot blight,
And in the radiant morning
  We'll forget the darksome night.

And so I sit here dreaming
  In the calm and quiet night,
Of the sad, sweet memories of the past
  And the future, fair and bright.
Then softly doth Oblivion draw
  Her mystic veil between,
And shuts out the haunting memories
  Of that happy Hallowe'en.

Thanksgiving.

Thank God for Life !
E'en tho' it bring much bitterness and strife,
  And all our fairest hopes be wrecked and lost ;
E'en tho' there be more ill than good in Life
  We cling to Life and reckon not the cost.
      Thank God for Life.

Thank God for Love !
For tho' sometimes Grief follows in its wake,
  Still we forget Love's sorrow in Love's joy
And cherish tears with smiles for Love's dear sake ;
  Only in Heaven is bliss without alloy.
      Thank God for Love.

Thank God for Pain !
No tear hath ever yet been shed in vain,
  And in the end each sorrowing heart shall find
No curse, but blessings in the hand of Pain ;
  Even when He smiteth, then is God most kind.
      Thank God for Pain.

Thank God for Death !
Who touches anguished lips and stills their breath,
  And giveth Peace unto each troubled breast ;
Grief flies before thy touch, O blessed Death !
  God's sweetest gift ; thy name in Heaven is Rest.
      Thank God for Death.

My Prayer.

Ye who have struggled with me in the strife,
   Ye who have braved the conflict, fought and bled,
My comrades on the battle-field of Life,
   Deal with me gently after I am dead.

Remember not my many frailties,
   My faults and failings, though they are not few,
Nay, countless as the sands beside the seas,
   Still would I ask forgetfulness from you.

It may be that some comrade's heart hath bled,
   Sore wounded by some careless shaft of mine,
But let not anger live against the dead,
   " To err is human, to forgive Divine."

And if your wrath is fierce and fain would live,
   Remember that I also suffered wrong,
Yet found it in my power to forgive.
   Though Hate is mighty, Love is still more strong.

One virtue I can surely call my own,
   Perchance, with it, my life has not been vain ;
My ears were swift to hear another's moan,
   My eyes were swift to weep for others' pain.

So when you breathe my name in future years
  Deal gently with the comrade who is gone,
Remember her as one who shared your tears
  And felt your sorrows even as her own.

O friends ! Deny me not the boon I ask,
  Is human wrath more dread than that of Heaven ?
Is pardoning a fault so great a task
  That man should dare refuse what God has given ?

Trace all my frailties in Oblivion's sand,
  But grave my virtues deep on memory's shrine ;
When this is done by Heaven's recording hand
  Can human hearts refuse this prayer of mine ?